DON'T MAKE ME LAUGH

When separated baby twins Leo and Trevor are reunited 27 years later, it's a cause of celebration.

That is until Leo accuses his brother of sleeping with his woman. Now they are brothers at arms.

Only their newly found mother can stop them ripping each other to bits. But HER terrible secret from the past means that one of them has to die.

DON'T MAKE ME LAUGH

Patrick Augustus

LARGE
PRINT

First published in 2006 by
The X Press
This Large Print edition published
2006 by BBC Audiobooks by
arrangement with
The X Press

ISBN 1 4056 2199 0
ISBN 13: 978 1 405 62199 1

British Library Cataloguing in Publication Data available

Printed and bound in Great Britain by the MPG Books Group

1

LEO'S STORY

My brother got off with my wife. He thinks I don't know, but I do. He thinks he's got away with it. But he hasn't. You wait and see. You can't have it off with your brother's wife and escape with no trouble. Stuff like that bites you back. It's called karma. If you spit in the sky it will fall in your eye. No doubt.

My brother Trevor had it off with my wife but you wouldn't think it to hear him singing.

'We're gonna win the cup. We're gonna win the cup. Ee-yay-addee-oh. We're gonna win the cup.'

Like he hasn't got a care in the world. Like I'm not standing next to him with a razor in my pocket and murder on my mind. I'm going to slit his throat.

We turn the turnstiles at White Hart Lane with thousands of other football fans. Trevor is chanting *'We're gonna win the cup. We're gonna win the cup. Ee-yay-addee-oh. We're gonna win the cup!'*

He's jumping up and down and slapping me on my back. Like me and him are friends. We might be brothers, but I'm no friend of Trevor's. Love and hate can never be friends. Trevor may be my brother, but I'm still going to cut off his balls.

You see Trevor's not just my brother, he's my twin. We're supposed to be tight. Like glue. From head to toe. Dusk till dawn. Cradle to grave. Same blood, same heart. One love. Til death do us part. We should be feeling each other. Fighting for each other. Beef with Trevor should be beef with me.

We're supposed to be peas in a pod. He's my other half. We're a matching pair. Same difference. Except we're not. We're opposites.

2

He's black and I'm white. He's in the wrong and I'm in the right. He's a dead man.

'We're gonna win the cup, Leo. Can you believe it. I'm telling you, it's gonna to be one long party. We're gonna win the cup. Then the league. Then the Champions League. We're gonna win the bloody lot.'

I stare at Trevor without blinking. He's right. We've had a brilliant season. The best ever. But I'm not cheering and I don't feel like talking. I'm killing time.

Once I would have killed for Trevor. I had a lot of love for him. That's how it is when you find your other half. You're strong. Like nothing could ever go wrong. Then your other half kicks you in the groin, whacks you across the bridge of the nose with a baseball bat and stabs you in the heart. That's how it feels. All because of my brother.

Out of all the women in the world

he couldn't stop himself from having sex with my wife.

We ought to be partners not rivals. Trevor and me. We should have been watching out for each other. We could have achieved so much between us. There's so much to say still not said. So much love still not loved. I would have gone to hell for him. Now, I just want to send him there.

2

LEO'S STORY

I never even knew I had a twin until a year ago. The first of April. I'll never forget it. It was a Sunday. One of those sunny, lazy mornings. I jogged down the road to get the morning papers. Can you believe my shock when I saw myself staring back at me from the front page of one of the tabloids?

*HAVE-A-GO HERO IN JAIL
SHAME*

The headline screamed. I panicked, snatched at the paper and scanned the story.

*HAVE-A-GO HERO IN JAIL
SHAME
The have-a-go hero who foiled a*

daring bank robber has a prison record as long as his arm, it has been revealed.

30-year-old Trevor Dunkley was jailed . . .

I bought the paper. In fact I bought as many papers as I could and jogged back home to read more.

HAVE-A-GO HERO IN JAIL SHAME

The have-a-go hero who foiled a daring bank robber has a prison record as long as his arm, it has been revealed.

30-year-old Trevor Dunkley was jailed for his role in a con that could have netted £1m from a top West End casino . . .

As you can imagine I was stunned. My heart was racing. *30-year-old Trevor Dunkley*. I read the words over and over again. I looked at the picture. My spitting image. A different surname but the same age as me. What are the chances of it being a fluke? All sorts of things were going through my head. All of them bad.

To be honest I was scared. It crossed my mind that it was April Fool's Day. Perhaps someone was having a laugh. Perhaps this was all some fancy hoax. Perhaps the paper seller was in on it too. Perhaps even the News of the World were winding me up. What are the chances of that?

*   *   *

Back in the stadium, it's three on the dot. Kick-off time. The noise of the White Hart Lane crowd is like the roar of the sea in a storm. The fans are screaming their heads off. But I may as well be deaf to it. I'm thinking too deeply about my brother's stinky-breath tongue in my wife's mouth. What about his dirty cock?

The more I think about it, the more angry I become. The ref blows his whistle, but all I can hear is Trevor singing, 'We're gonna win the cup! We're gonna win the cup' while sexing my wife. Who is winning? Who is losing? Who is in white and who is in blue? Whose throw-in is that? Whose corner? Free-kick? Penalty? Who cares?

'That was never a penalty, ref!' I hear the fans jeer. What do I know? My mind is somewhere else. Even if it had been the Cup Final the moaning of my wife making love to my brother would have drowned out the roar of the crowd.

Trevor nudges me in the ribs all friendly. I swear to God if he does that again I'll slit both his wrists and end this bullshit here and now.

'Oi Leo. What's the matter, Bruv? We're one-nil up and you ain't said a peep. You haven't even moved. What's up? Are you watching the same game I'm looking at? We just scored. Or is your mind on some other type of scoring? Only birds can have that effect on a bloke in the middle of a great match. Is there something you want to tell me, Bruv? Have you been having it off with some skirt on the sly? Is that what's up?'

He winked at me. I could have boxed him.

'I'm a married man,' I said through gritted teeth. 'Or did you forget?'

*   *   *

When I first found out about Trevor and my wife I refused to believe it. Even though the proof was staring me in the face. If I had been there in the room with them and seen it myself, I would have still doubted my eyes. I would have thought I was dreaming. That's what this feels like, a horrible dream.

Like the nightmares I've been having all my life. It's always the same dream. The falling off the edge of a cliff one where you wake up just before you hit the ground. Only it isn't me falling. It's someone else. A man. Tall. With a moustache. Always well dressed. Always wearing a trilby. Always reaching out for me as he falls backwards. Always laughing his head off as he vanishes over the edge of the cliff.

The same dream. Every night. As far back as I recall. The same dream. Every bloody night. Without fail.

I don't talk about it. I'm too ashamed. Too afraid of how it would make me look and what people would say. Would they think I was a nutter who needed help? I mean, it's weird isn't it? Having the same bloody dream every damn night. They would send me to a shrink and before you know it, I would start to sink with all the drugs the quacks give you. If you want to get on in the police force you can't afford to let people know your true mental state.

We're gonna win the cup
We're gonna win the cup
Eee-eye-addee-o
We're gonna win the cup.

It's that dream again. It's a hot day. Somewhere out in the country. There's a picnic with people eating and laughing. I am a toddler crawling through the grass. Away from the others. In the distance I can see a ship. It looks a lot closer than it is. I am moving towards it knowing that danger lies ahead. Even in my dreams I am begging the young me not to crawl any further.

I must have been as stubborn as an infant as I am now. I carry on. But someone grabs me by the hand and shoves me from behind. I go hurtling over the cliff screaming. On my way down the endless abyss I realise it's not me. It's that mystery man again. The tall one with the moustache. Wearing a trilby. Yet again I am

11

confused. What does it all mean? Why do I keep getting these dreams? Who is that man? Is it my father? And who was it who pushed me over the cliff?

3

LEO'S STORY

I can't believe murder is on my mind all the time. I swear to God I feel like death is calling me.

My brother and my wife. How do you expect me to feel? Angry. Sad. Bitter.

Twisted. Shocked. Angry. Angry. Angry. How would you feel?

I can see it in her eyes.

Trevor's a good actor. But Jenny isn't. Her eyes don't lie. The very first time she looked at me I knew I was in with a chance.

At the time, she was a waitress in a bar. It wasn't the most romantic place. But that didn't bother me. It felt like a magic carpet ride.

I fancied her right away. And her eyes told me, 'try your luck'.

I could read her mind just by looking into her eyes. She was like an open book. Deep in her eyes I could see what she was thinking.

I still can. That's why she can't look me in the face any longer. Not the way she used to.

I was crazy about Jenny. You won't believe this but my heart went zing, zing, zing the moment I saw her. It had never done that before. I knew straight away that I wanted to marry her. People said I was rushing things, moving too fast. But I knew she was the woman for me. I was in romance heaven until my brother came out of jail and couldn't stop himself from sleeping with her.

My blood is boiling. I'm waiting to explode with my boot in my cheating brother's bollocks. He betrayed me. Just when I thought I had found my soul-mate. Someone I could trust with my life. Someone I could rely on. He used my love and slept with my wife. I'll castrate him.

'YEEEEEEEEE-HA! We're gonna win the bloody lot!' Trevor screams, pumping his hands up and down and dancing a jig. 'YEEEEEEEEE-HA!'

We've just scored again and the crowd at White Hart Lane are ready to party. We have not quite won the tie yet though. They've also scored. The ref has added two minutes of extra time. The game could still end in a draw. But I don't care.

With 90 seconds to go the ball is in the air and seems to hang there for ages. The sun is shining bright in the sky. I look up. All I can see is red. Red mist. All I can hear is my wife and my brother panting.

Their heavy breathing all mixed up. Loud and getting louder. It echoes. Like there are three lots of my wife and three lots of my brother screaming 'Yes. Yes. Yesssssss. JEEZAS CRIES! Yes. Yes.

Yesssssss.'

My brother did the nasty with my wife and I'm feeling it bad. D'you get me? How could he do it? I keep asking myself. How could he betray me like that? Could he do it without thinking about me? Was he able to do it while thinking about me? I must have been on his mind the whole time he was on top of her. Or was she on top of him? How could he blank me out? No one is that cold. Are they?

I felt like telling Trevor there and then 'You think I don't know. You think I'm blind. You think I'm stupid. You think you're so clever? Well you're not. I've sussed you and I'm going to sort you. You wait and see.'

But I didn't.

We're going to win the cup, but I can't stop thinking of my dirty brother in bed with my woman. Him inside her. Making me sick. Did he go down on her or did she? Did he take her from behind or up front?

16

Why do I need to know?

Half the stadium is chanting 'Who's the bastard in the black!!' But all I can hear is the groan of sexual pleasure. Louder and louder. Harder and harder. Longer and longer. My brother riding my wife like a jockey. YEEEEEEEEE-HA like a cowboy.

I reached for the blade in my pocket. I could so easily stick it through his windpipe here and now.

I'm not sure any longer if Trevor is really still singing or whether I'm just hearing things. Like Kylie, I just can't get it out of my head. We're gonna win the cup! We're gonna win the cup, ee-yay-addee-oh we're gonna win the cup!

The thought of my brother and my wife is making me sick. Really sick. I can feel the puke climbing up my throat. Like I'm going to throw up at any moment. From the bottom of my stomach. Bile. Is that what they call it? I'm not sure. All I know is I can taste it creeping up the back of my throat. And it tastes vile.

I FEEL sick. But Trevor's the one who's not well. You've got to be sick to have sex with your brother's wife. Sick upstairs. He needs his head tested. Yeah, tested against my boot. I'll kick his head in.

I should kill him here and now. I should strangle him. I could beat him to death with my bare hands. That's how I feel. That's why I'm sticking two fingers down my throat to make Trevor feel how I feel.

HERE COMES THE BILE.

In Trevor's lap.

'Ahhhh shit, Leo! What the frigg you have to do that for?'

'Sorry,' I smile. 'Not feeling too well.'

'But there's thirty thousand other people here. Why did it have to be me? Why the f......'

Before Trevor completes what he had to say a huge roar goes up. It's another goal. Our section of the stadium is jumping for joy singing:

'We're gonna win the bloody lot!' Trevor is jumping up and down too. He didn't even see the goal. But nothing else seems to matter.

As for the vomit, he wipes his jeans on the coat of the man in front.

*   *   *

After seeing Trevor's picture in the papers last year I didn't know what to do. I was confused. My cop instincts were weighing up the facts. My common sense was telling me that I should leave it well alone. That this was a can of worms. I might regret looking into it. I checked police records at the station and found out a bit more about this 'have a go hero'. There was quite a lot on him.

He lived not far from me. He had been passing-by when he noticed a robber inside the bank. He had waited outside the door and as the man with the loot made his get-away,

19

Trevor had stuck his foot out and the villain had gone flying.

One moment Trevor was a hero and the next he went back down to zero when the tabloids found out about his time behind bars.

I must have been staring at the paper for hours. I read the story over and over. I couldn't get it off my mind. I couldn't stop glaring at the photo of me staring back at me. In the end I picked up the phone and called the last person on earth.

4

LEO'S STORY

She agreed to meet up in a Little Chef on the M1. It was the day after I saw Trevor's picture in the papers. By then I had worked things out for myself. Lady Charles pulled up in a flash, chauffeur driven Merc.

She climbed out dressed in a full length fur coat with a pearl necklace around her throat.

Mum was the last person on earth I wanted to ask. I don't know about Trevor but I can't forgive her for not being there for me all these years. What kind of a mother would give up her kids? I've heard all her reasons but I still say she should have kept her boys with her. She shouldn't have vanished like that. And what sort of a mother would allow her kids to be split up? Not just any kids, but twins.

21

I want to hate her but I can't. She's still my mother no matter what she's done. There's nothing I can do to change things. That's life. I can't hate her for passing her children around like a cold. Somebody did somebody wrong here. But I'm still not mad at her.

She joined me at my table, as usual with one eye on the door ready to dash out again. She said she could only a stay a while and declined a coffee. She was always in a hurry. Never had time to stick around. It's the story of our lives.

'Mum, why didn't you tell me I had a brother?' I asked.

She cleared her throat.

'I'm sorry you had to find out this way. Listen my love, stay away from him. Take my advice, Trevor's no good. He is a bad boy. From youth. The black sheep. In and out of prison always doing wrong. Your brother is the last person on earth you need in your life. You are doing so well. I am so proud of you. I follow your progress with a glow in my heart. I've done so all these years. Ever since you were a little boy. Even though you didn't know.

'I knew that you had passed your exams at school. I knew you had joined the police force. You were doing so well, I wasn't going to let your brother spoil that. What you didn't know didn't hurt you.'

'You shouldn't have split us up in the first place.' I told her.

'I wish I hadn't. But I didn't mean to. It hurt me to do it. It broke my heart. It still hurts today. Like I keep telling you over and over, it was a struggle back then. Your dad left us without a penny. The stress got to me. I didn't know what I was doing. I didn't know where to turn.

'I could not manage two children on my own. I had no choice. No mother should have to choose between her sons. But I did. To save us. I chose you. I've always loved you

Leo. You were my youngest child. "My little man" I used to call you. Even though you were only a baby.

'When the doctor told me I was having a breakdown, I knew I had to give you up as well. I tried to find the people who took Trevor to see if they would take you too. But they had moved abroad. So I did my best to look after you until the day you nearly died. That's when I had no choice but to give you up too. For your own good and safety.

'I had been sitting in front of the telly doing nothing all day. You hadn't even crossed my mind until I had to go upstairs to the loo. That's when I saw you balanced on the window ledge, about to fall down. Somehow you had managed to crawl onto the toilet seat and lean out. I caught you in the nick of time. I snatched you from the jaws of death. I saved your life, Leo. Don't forget that. You wouldn't be here if it wasn't for me.

'That explains those bad dreams you told me about. That's where they come from. It's you falling over the cliff in that dream, and it nearly happened. Except it wasn't a cliff. It was upstairs at our old house.

'You see, don't you, why I had to give you up. It was to protect you. I didn't want to neglect you. It was through the doctor that I met the vicar's wife. She had been trying to have a baby for years. She offered you a good home. And she did keep her promise to bring you up as if you were her own son. It was in your best interest. An offer I could not refuse.'

When she puts it like that what can you say? Thanks for splitting us up? No. What could I say? I couldn't argue. It all sounded like Mum did the right thing. I almost felt sorry for her. Except that I know the truth. She doesn't know I know, but I do.

You see, when my other parents (the vicar and his wife) died in a car crash two years ago, I was left to go

25

through their things. Isn't it strange how we keep certain things private and our deepest thoughts to ourselves. Yet the moment you die, the very second you pass away, your whole life is exposed to the world. All your secrets are out.

My other mother had a big secret. I stumbled across it as I was going through her papers and sorting out what to throw away and what to keep. I nearly binned it. It looked like a scrap of paper, an old piece of paper that had faded yellow. But when I took a closer look I noticed it was a bill of sale. A receipt:

Received by Maria Hibbert, the sum of £5,000 in receipt of Leonard Hibbert.

That was all. I couldn't understand it at first. But it didn't take long for me to add two and two and make four. I'm a cop, adding is what I do for a living. The date on the receipt was the clincher. I would have been two years old. Which must have been the same time the vicar and his wife took me in.

Up until I found that scrap of paper I had never known who my real mother was. When I asked, the vicar's wife said I was a 'gift from God'.

'I should have taken you to the police,' she used to say, 'but your mother begged me to bring you up as my own son. It was her last wish.'

So I always believed my mother was dead. But she was very much alive. I tracked down Maria Hibbert through the police computer. When I saw her I knew straight away she was my mum.

It would have been so easy to produce my proof of sale. But I didn't and haven't. That's my secret weapon if ever I need to use it. My mother sold me for £5,000. And maybe my brother too. That's what Lady Charles will have to answer to.

When the right time comes.

All the nonsense she says about not having any choices is just crap. Five grand? No choices? Don't me laugh.

She got up to leave the café.

'By the way, did you go and see that healer about your dream?' she asked.

'The witch doctor? Yes. But I don't know if it helped. I've started dreaming in the daytime as well now.'

'Oh dear,' she said.

'It's him isn't it, the trilby, the moustache, tall, slim, it's my dad isn't it?'

'How could it be? How would you know? You've never seen him. You were just a baby when he walked out. He left us to die. That is why I burned every photo of him.'

'I know that it's my father. I can see it in his face. When I look in his eyes I see my soul looking back at me. It's my dad all right. It couldn't be any other person.'

28

'Leave it alone, Leo. Stop thinking like that. If you want the dreams to stop the last thing you want is to start studying them. You need to forget. Even if it is your dad in the dream, what does it matter? He's been gone nearly thirty years. You don't know where he is.'

'Yes I do.'

'You found him?' She looked puzzled.

'I've checked police records,' I said. 'I've tracked him down to a housing estate in Luton.'

5

LEO'S STORY

It was pouring down with rain when I arrived at the leafy avenue in Luton that Sunday afternoon. The woman who answered kept me standing in the rain.

Yes, a Harry Hibbert did live there, she told me. 'But I don't think he's your father. He's my son. And he's not much older than you.'

I asked several more questions. I described the Harry Hibbert I was looking for. Tall. Slim. With a thin moustache. Used to wear a trilby hat.

Her arms were folded across her chest. She simply shook her head.

Drenched to the skin I thanked her and turned to go.

'He was a bastard, you know.'

I spun round.

'Your dad. He was a bastard,' she

said again. 'He left me alone with a baby. That was thirty years ago. I haven't seen him since.'

This time I wasn't shocked to hear that I had another brother I had never met. Who knows? There might be others. Nothing can surprise me any more. I'm not even bothered about meeting him. All I wanted was a photo of him. Something to help me track him down. She couldn't help me.

'There was a photo once but Junior had burned it in a fit of rage at the father who had never been there. The father who was the spitting image of him.'

She went indoors and returned with a photo of her son but she wouldn't let me keep it. A handsome lad about my age. He was in uniform. A cop too. But it was his face I couldn't stop looking at. That was the face in my dreams. He even had the moustache. The only thing missing was the trilby.

So I know what my father looks like. I mean, I feel I know him really well. Like I've seen him every day of my life. In a way I have. In my dreams. I've got a photo-fit of him in my head. I know who I'm looking for. I just don't know where to look. I've followed several leads and have come up with nothing. I've checked the records over and over. Nothing. Even if he was dead, there should be some record of it. It's like my dad has vanished off the face of the earth.

Someone somewhere has got the answer to this mystery. I need to find out who. But all I can think about is my dirty brother sticking his filthy thing into my missus. I need to sort him out first.

6

TREVOR'S STORY

'Hey Bruv, can you believe it, we've won the cup, we've won the cup, ee-yay-addee-oh, we've won the cup. Thanks to my great goal. You've got to admit it was pure skill. The goal of the season. I dribbled two players and nutmegged a third before blasting it into the corner of the net with my weaker left foot. Can you believe I scored in the last minute of the five-a-side Sunday League Cup.

'I thought you would be cheering too, Leo? You looked gutted. Or was you just knackered after running up and down the pitch for an hour? Yeah, well get some of this brandy down you. It will put some iron in your rod. I mean, you can't get done for drinking and driving, can you? You're a cop.

'Bruv, I love this. Me and you hanging out. Cruising in your motor? It's great. Nice set of wheels, by the way.

'This is what I've always wanted. Nothing more than to just kick it with my Bruv. It feels good to say the word. Bruv.

'But I need to know, Bruv, where we stand with each other. Do we share this special thing called "love"? I know I do. What about you? Cause I've got plans, Bruv. Big plans. And you figure big in my plans. It's me and you, Bruv. Against the world. You get me?

'And look at the amount of women out there. Two for every man. Boom-boom-boom. You'll soon get your first cap. Humping for England. In midfield.

'I loooooooove you, Bruv. I loooooooove ya. I really do. Yeah, I've had a few, but I'm not drunk. Hic. I'm just tipsy. There's no law against that is there? You tell me.

You're the cop. Can't a man go and get a little sloshed?

'I hope we get a chance to talk proper, Bruv. Because we need to get to know each other. To make up for all these lost years. You see, I've been having this dream . . . I don't know what it means. I can't explain. But it's the same dream.'

7

TREVOR'S STORY

What do I know about the old man?

I only know that he is the bastard who left us when we were just babies. Why would I waste time thinking of him. I don't care if that bastard is dead. I would still piss on his grave. If I ever saw him, I wouldn't be able to stop myself from spitting in his face. All of this is all his fault. He was the one who left his children and ran off with some other woman. He was the one. If he hadn't run off with some woman, mum wouldn't have had to give us away because she couldn't afford to keep us.

We would have grown up in the same house. We would have been happy. So no, I don't think about him. When I think about him at all I get very angry. Like I want to do something bad. Like I want to kill someone.

You know, when I was a kid people would come up to me sometimes and go on about something I didn't have a clue about. Now when I think about it, they must have thought I was you Bruv. Perhaps you had the same problem too?

There was this one time, at school, when I was coming back from games, yeah, and these guys jumped me. They told me to give them the money I owed them or they would stab me up there and then. They wasn't kidding either.

They cut me with a razor when I couldn't pay up. Here's the scar to prove it. All down my arm. Now I'm thinking maybe it was you they was looking for. Was you really a bad boy back in those days, Bruv?

The joke about it is that I always wished I had a brother. You know, someone to kick around with. A buddy to rely on. Someone watching out for me. A soul-mate I could trust with my life. Someone I would die for.

Yes, I always wished I had a brother, but a brother who is old bill was the last thing on earth I would have wished for. I mean, me and the cops don't see eye-to-eye. We never have. Cops and me haven't got on well since I was a kid. Back in those days they used to give you a clip round the earhole for being cheeky. At first we was only larking around, breaking windows, playing 'knock down ginger' and scrumping for apples over garden walls.

But after one too many clips round the lughole I started turning bad. Real bad. It was pure hard times. That's why I was always getting into trouble.

I was only seven when I started nicking. Sweets and stuff. Look, I didn't have much when I was growing up. You was lucky. The people you lived with could afford to give you the best. The folks I lived with were hardly ever there. They didn't give me jack. They left me to fend for myself. Sometimes I didn't have any money. So I had to rob and steal when I was hungry. Are you with me? I went to school with salt and pepper in my pocket. No lie.

But I thought I had the master plan. I was breaking into cars at ten. And in and out of borstal in my teens. Like I said, if I knew I had a brother who was into law and order, none of that might have happened.

Maybe I always knew I had a brother, Bruv. You see, I saw you once, Leo. When we was seven-years-old. I'll never forget it. And I'm sure you saw me too. It was on a Sunday morning back when there used to be a lido on Lordship Lane. Me and a couple of kids from our estate was going swimming. We had bunked on the bus, the one that goes through the posh part of our area. It goes past that fancy church with a tower and turrets on the corner of the High Street. As the bus waited at the traffic lights I looked across at the people going in to pray. And there you was, standing out front next to the vicar.

It was like seeing a ghost. I didn't know you was my brother. But I knew you was my twin. I know it sounds funny. But that's how you feel when you see your spitting image for the first time. I knew you was my other half. A part of me I didn't even know was missing. I was scared. You really spooked me. I didn't know what to do. I didn't know who this boy was and I was too afraid of what I might find if I looked.

I don't know why, but I sort of half-waved. That's when I figured you must have seen me because you looked up to the top deck and kind of waved too. But you seemed to change your mind. Like you thought better of it.

You must have seen me. Your look

changed from love to hate. You screwed your face into a scowl. I think you stuck your tongue out at me but I'm not sure.

I never told a soul about it. All these years. And that's not the only thing that's been on my mind. I'll tell you about my dreams later.

So I didn't go near that church again. I stayed away from your part of town. Besides I had no business over that side. I didn't know you or any other person who lived there and I never went to the lido again. Ever.

I clocked you once more though. When I was maybe nine or ten. One time when a fair pitched up in the woods on my side. I was having a laugh on the dodgem cars when I saw you. You was on the Wurlitzer screaming your head off. I watched you whiz by a couple of times to be sure it was you. I felt like going up to you and asking you who did you think you was. I should have punched you on the nose for even being there. Instead of that I got out of the car and ran all the way home crying.

I never saw you again. I was in and out of borstal for years after that. For this and that. Sometimes for sweet FA. Borstal to prison was like school to college. In and out, in and out. Same gates, same mates.

There was this one time though when I was doing time in the Scrubs. This new inmate arrives, an old timer, giving me an evil look.

'Don't I know you?' he said.

I had never seen him before in my life.

'Yes, I know you.' He didn't give up. 'You're old bill.'

I laughed my head off.

But he was convinced. He wouldn't let it go.

'You nicked me last year. Credit card fraud. YOU'RE OLD BILL.'

He raised his voice with every word.

It didn't take long for a circle of

guys to form around me.

The last thing on my mind was that maybe that boy who looked just like me had grown up to be a cop and still looked just like me.

I shouted at the top of my voice. 'I've been here a year. How could I be filth? How could I have nicked you?'

The old con couldn't argue with that. He got friendly pats on the back and someone said he should think of going straight at his age with his mind going and all.

He still wasn't convinced though and throughout the rest of my time at the Scrubs the old villain kept one beady eye on me as if he was trying to figure out how I managed to pull off the con.

I kept myself to myself when he was around, which was nearly always. A prison's a small space. It's like living in the Big Brother house. Someone's watching you all the time. And if you don't get on with someone in there, well, you don't get on. The old lag kept coming up to me asking me questions like who my parents are, where I grew up, which cons I had done and how I had done them. The kind of questions you don't ask people when you're inside.

I wasn't happy about it. But what could I do? I knew he was fishing for clues, waiting for me to slip up. He was waiting in vain. So now years later I get to find out that my brother really is a cop! Ha! Can you believe it? Me, who was always being chased by the old bill down dark alleys and across rooftops.

I've even been in a car chase. But that was in the old days which was my younger days. I've done my time for the crimes and I've turned over a new leaf. Which is just as well, because my brother is a cop.

It takes a little getting used to, Bruv. I'll be honest. But I love you still, you know. You're my kid brother. By 90 seconds. And you support Spurs. Can you believe it? Even though we never knew each other we support the same team. That just goes to show you we've got a lot in common. Perhaps more than we realise. Yet we hardly know each other.

We're like strangers, even though we're twins. Neither of us really knows where the other is coming from. We don't share each other's secrets.

When we get to know each other a bit better it will become easy to be straight with each other. It takes a lot of guts to be honest, Bruv, but I just don't have the guts right now. I know this is all a bit much to take in, Bruv. But when you get to know me well enough you'll know that I would never do something to hurt you. You can depend on me like my name was Patches.

You're my brother. When you bleed I bleed. I feel your hurt. It pains me too. I share your success.

And I have to bear your failures. Whether I like it or not. That's the way it is with brothers. Believe me. Brothers may fight with each other, but they won't kill each other. They don't knock each other's blocks off. They fight, argue then get over it. Sometimes it makes them stronger. Tighter. Like glue.

8

TREVOR'S STORY

Bruv, we never met, yet we was going to the same ground to cheer on the same team week after week. Can you dig it?

Like I say, we're alike in so many ways. Even though we didn't know each other. It's in the genes, I guess. I've got nine inches in mine. I suppose you've got the same in your jeans. We are twins after all. After all we've been through, Bruv, isn't it a relief that we're well endowed. That was the one thing that bastard father of ours left us. Nine inches of pleasure. The ladies love it. One taste is all it takes and they're hooked.

But I'm sure you know how to make a woman moan with delight too, don't you? I'm sure you got plenty of panty action before you tied the knot. Isn't it great to know you can make any girl holler and scream, moan and groan with delight?

So what do you prefer, a woman with a big behind to hold on to or a woman with big breasts? No, come on. Really. Are you a breast man or a bum man?

I'm just trying to get to know you, Bruv.

I mean, check that woman walking over there. Yeah. The one with the lips and them hips. Slow down, Bruv. Slow down.

Pssst! Pssssst!

'Hey girl, you wanna ride with Mr Rock Steady. That's what the ladies call me. I'd like to show you why.

'What's that, girl? What do you mean where's my girl? She's with your man. So let me take you home and make it up to you?

'Hey, calm down, girl. Your pretty face don't match your ugly mouth, ya know. Yeah-yeah, you too. With knobs on.'

You see that, Bruv. What did I tell you. She wants it. You saw that, right? Gagging for it. Didn't I tell you I know more about women than they know about themselves. That's what being banged up with hundreds of guys does to you. All you think about is the female of the species.

Every woman you've ever known, every woman you've ever come across and every woman you've ever seen or ever heard of. From your childhood sweetheart to the mother you hardly know. You try to figure them out. Over and over in your mind. Until you know every single thing about them, better than than they know themselves.

I know what makes them tick. And I know what makes them tock. Ha-ha! You get it? I know what makes them come and what makes them go. That's what women tell me.

I've spent too much of my life

banged up, Bruv. I'm making up for lost banging time. You get me? That's why I can't stick to one woman.

I mean, check that girl standing over there. See the way she's giving me the eye. How can I resist? Pull up, Bruv. Pull up to the kerb. Let me lean out the window.

'Hey girl, it's me and you tonight, baby! I'll fly you to the moon. You get me?

'Oh, is that your man? I didn't know he was so huge. No offence, mate. I was just keeping an eye on your girl, while you was having a slash. Yeah. Any time, mate.'

Drive on, Bruv. Drive. Put your foot down.

Phew!

Talk about close shaves, Bruv. Believe me I've had a few. I met this lady one time. Big tits and big batty. She had a ring on her finger so I knew what was what. We went over to her house when her husband was at work. Ya know what I mean?

So there I am giving it the full slam but it takes her so long to come that a few hours went by in minutes. I wiped the sweat from my eyes. Then I hear the front door slam and a deep voice boom, 'Baby, daddy's home.'

It's her husband. Well, I didn't hang about to explain what I was doing in bed with his missus. I grabbed my pants, put on my Kangol and I was out of there. It was a bathroom window jobby. Me hanging from the ledge naked. Not for the first time.

Here's the joke though. The woman in question keeps begging me for more. She hasn't learned her lesson. She's out of control. She's crying down the phone. Says I teased her out of her mind. And now she wants me to finish the job I started. In her bedroom. Man, I tell you, married women are the hardest to please.

Hey Bruv, take it easy. You nearly knocked down that old man. What's the matter. Your eyes are like daggers. You look like you could kill somebody.

Hey, Bruv. D'you hear me? Slow down. You'll crash the car if you're not careful. And Bruv, I think you're going the wrong way.

9

TREVOR'S STORY

Aaaaaaaaaaaaaaaagh!!!!!!!!
What the fuck. What the fuck did you do that for? Why the fuck d'you have to headbutt me?

I'm sorry, I didn't mean to break your nose with my elbow, but you hit me first, Bruv. I didn't do nothing to you. So why did you have to frigging crack me with your head? Leo, I'm flipping talking to you. What's the matter with you? Why are you looking at me like you want to kill me? It's me, Trevor. Your long lost brother.

What the fuck is going on? Have you lost it or something? Have you gone crazy? Hey, put those fists down, or I'm going to have to break your hands, ya get me? We're in the frigging car. Parked on the frigging

53

road. This is no place to fight, but if you want beef, you'll get it. Hard.

There's something you should know about me before you try to take me on, Bruv. I've got a black belt in karate. So back the fuck off and give me respect.

Leo, d'you hear me? My hands and feet are deadly weapons. So calm down, Bruv and I'll loosen this armlock around your neck.

I don't want to hurt you. You've only got a broken nose, but I could have taken your head off with my elbow punch. So don't even try it.

Hey, Leo, I'm warning you. Don't make me have to lay another one on you. If I do, you won't forget it. So take it easy. You nearly got me in the bollocks with your knee. Try that again and, I swear, you're going to lose your balls.

Now listen to me, Bruv, and listen good. I don't know where you're coming from with all of this. I don't know what I've done to you. But we're supposed to be brothers. Brothers are supposed to work things out. That's what I always thought. We're not supposed to be knocking each other's block off. For any reason. Just because we didn't grow up together, we're still supposed to be tight.

Hey, what the frigg is that you've got in your hands. Damn it, what the fuck are you doing?

You're pushing it, Bruv. I'll smack the shit out of you. You are fucking up. Listen man . . .

Hey . . . Aaaaaaargh! It's burning. Aaaaaaaiiiiiieeeeeeeeeee. It's burning. What the fuck did you spray in my eyes? I've gone blind. You bastard. You've blinded me. I can't see. You stupid fucker. My eyes are burning.

Aaaaaaaiiiiiieeee.

Okay, you bastard. You asked for it. An eye for an eye. You want a fight. You've got one. You're wrong if you think I need to see you to kick your arse. It's just like boxing blindfold.

I'm used to it. You're going to feel it.

AAAAAIIIIIIIIIIIEEEEEEEEEE EEEEEE!!!!!

Okay, calm down. You're not dead yet. I've popped your eyeballs out of their sockets with my finger, that's all. They're dangling by your veins and a thread of muscle. That's why you're seeing me from your chin. You haven't lost your eyes yet, but you might lose them if you don't stop fighting and explain what's going on. I swear, I'm not joking now. I'll rip your eyeballs off and throw them out the car window. You'll never find them again. And then I'll break your neck. I swear.

I don't care if you are my twin brother. You see this headlock I've got you in, all I've got to do is tighten my grip a little and your neck will snap in two. Don't tempt me.

So be cool fool, don't even try and move. And if you love your life, you'll take a deep breath and tell me why you flipped.

What are you talking about, I fucked your wife?

Yes I know what it means.

But what do you mean?

It's kind of hard for me to look you in the eyes and say I didn't, isn't it? You've blinded me.

Did I or did I not have sex with your wife? What kind of question is that to ask.

No, it's not a simple question. You're my brother. You shouldn't be asking me that. You're supposed to trust me.

Have you asked your wife whether I slept with her?

No, I did not sleep with your wife. So you've blinded me for nothing.

Believe what you want but you'll see. If I don't yank your eyeballs off.

What makes you so sure I'm a 'frigging liar'?

Photos? What photos?

None of my business! You've

punched me and kicked me and blinded me. You nearly knocked me out with a head-butt, and you say it's none of my business.

Okay, you want to know the truth. Then let me lay my cards on the table.

First of all I saw her first. She and I met before she was your wife. Before you ever set eyes on her. Second, she didn't know I was your brother when she met you. I know people can't tell us apart. But that's how it was.

Yes, I expect you to believe that.

What you mean 'don't make me laugh'?

It's true.

Why don't you ask your wife yourself?

And even if I did get off with your wife, we're supposed to be twins. We're supposed to be tight. Like glue. From head to toe. Cradle to grave. My brother comes before my wife. That's how it is for me. If I got off with your wife there had to be a reason. It had to be a mistake. And it was. On the eve of your wedding.

Bruv, you have blinded me over a mistake. What kind of brother are you?

First of all I thought her name was Brenda. You see, it was only a one night stand. And after time behind bars I had mixed her up with some other girl.

It was the day I got out. Your stag night. I happened to be passing near her street. I thought of her. So I stopped by.

She buzzed me up. She didn't seem surprised to see me. Don't forget I had been inside. There was no way of me knowing this was the woman you were going to marry.

'Yo, you look tired,' I said.

She said, 'Yeah, I did the late shift.'

It was late.

I said, 'I hope you don't mind me coming round like this.

She was like, 'No, why should I?'

She turned and went down the

dark hallway. I followed her into the bedroom. She was wearing a skimpy little nightdress that only reached to half way down her bum. I won't even lie to you, even though I was tired she was horny like hell.

She was so tired her eyes were closing the moment she was tucked back in between the sheets. But it was me, I was the one pushing for sex. She must have thought I was you. I know that now. Because she kept saying we've got all the time in our lives for this. She tried to push me away, still not knowing that I was I and not you. People can't tell us apart when they're wide awake, Bruv, so how do you reckon someone who is half-asleep is going to know that I'm not you? And yeah, we made love.

What's happened has happened. All one big mistake. You should know that. There's nothing I can do about it. It's no-one's fault. That's just the way it is.

10

THE WIFE'S STORY

'Let me ask you a question, Jen. You ever sleep around on me?'

I can't believe what I just heard. I look deep in his eyes to see where the question is coming from. My search for a clue is in vain.

'No, of course not,' I said after a while. 'Why would I do that?'

'But you had to think about it. What took you so long to answer?'

'I don't know. I was just thinking about the question.'

He looks at me with a look that says 'tell that to some fool who believes you.'

'Okay, let me ask you one more question. You know what crimes of passion are?'

I nod.

'Good,' he says. 'Because if I ever,

EVER catch you screwing around, I won't be in control of my actions. I'm not playing. This isn't a joke. If I catch you with some guy, I'll cut his dick off. I swear to God I will. Who knows what I'd do to you. I'm a jealous guy.'

It's more like a threat than a warning. Like he knows. I have never seen Leo like this before. His eyes are red. It looks like he has not slept for days. But he seems deadly serious. What the hell is going on?

If he already knows, why is he making threats? Why has he not acted?

*   *   *

As the song goes, I was working as a waitress in a cocktail bar when I met him. It was one of those rainy days which brings in all kinds of people off the street.

I noticed him straightaway the moment he entered. There was

something about him. I'm not sure what.

He noticed me straightaway too. Our eyes met across the bar. Only briefly. But long enough for him to be hooked.

Then I looked away, past him, through the door he had just come through and out onto the street outside. I don't know why. It was an intense few moments. It was like he had me in his power. Even with my eyes fixed on the passers-by in the rain outside. All I could think about was making love to this complete stranger who had just come in. I could feel his stare even though I wasn't looking.

Then he spoke to me with the gift of the gab.

'You're killing me softly with those eyes of yours.'

Did he say that or was that me?

And that smile.

It was the most beautiful thing I had ever seen on a human face.

Even now when I think about it, it sounds like I'm going over the top. No one is really that perfect.

It's all about timing.

I was ready for him. He came into my life when I had dreamt about love for a long time. I had had a few boyfriends. But had never been in love. He was different. The moment he walked through the door it felt like he was the one I had been waiting for. I took his order. A rum and coke.

'It's on the house,' I said.

I was possessed. I must have been. Why else would I risk my job by giving free drinks. I really didn't care. That's what I wanted to do for him. He looked up, not even surprised. Like he had had no intention of paying. Like that kind of thing happens to him every day. He raised his glass and read my name badge.

'Jenny, cheers,' he said.

He never took his eyes off me

once. Even when my back was turned I could feel his eyes burning into me.

He asked me for my number before he left. Like a robot I wrote it on the back of a napkin. He smiled his charming smile and told me to expect him.

I hurried home after my shift. I couldn't wait for him to call. He didn't call, but showed up at my flat with a bunch of roses shortly after I arrived.

He must have followed me home but I didn't have time to ask. Because as soon as I answered the door he planted a kiss on my lips. A proper kiss. A long and probing kiss. A kiss I couldn't resist.

He stood at my door smiling that smile. I couldn't resist.

That night we made pure love. Perfect love. Real love. It was the best. I could have gone on all night. In fact, I may have done. It was love without an end. It just seemed to go on and on.

The next morning he was gone. No number. No note. Just gone. As if he had never been there. Except he had. There was his smell. The smell of great sex. And he had taken my spare key.

I hoped he would use it. I hoped and I hoped and I hoped. For weeks and weeks and weeks. Even if I had waited years, the door to my heart would have stayed open for Trevor. So you can guess how I felt when he walked back into my life?

It was two years later. I was still working as a waitress in the cocktail bar. He stepped in out of the rain. He saw me straight away and for a moment he watched me watching him. He smiled and winked at me and then called me over. I could have cursed him.

He acted like he didn't know me. Two years might have passed but I could remember that night like it was yesterday. I could even remember what drink he had. I poured a drink and snubbed him too. Even though my heart was dancing. Even though I was falling for him again.

For some reason he studied my name tag. 'Jenny,' he said, like it was the first time he was saying it, 'how did you know I was a rum and coke man?' He greeted me like we didn't know each other. Said his name was Leo.

I was thinking, Leo, Trevor, whatever. He was playing games. I played along.

He asked me if I 'come here often'.

I said 'Ha ha, very funny. I work here, so it's a stupid question.'

'You're a Virgo,' he said.

'And I bet you're a Leo,' I replied.

'Good guess,' he said.

'Likewise,' I said.

Then he asked me out. I said 'deja-vu'.

He said 'What?'

I said, it's French. It means 'haven't I been here before?'

'In another life?' he asked.

67

I was like, 'Yeah, whatever'. I gave him my number. Again. My heart told me to.

11

THE WIFE'S STORY

This time I made sure he took time to love. I didn't want no 'Wam bam thank you, ma'am'. This time I was going to make him fall in love. Trevor, Leo or whatever name he wanted to call himself, was the man for me.

He called my mobile every day. We talked for hours about nothing at all. Then we started going out. To the theatre. To the pictures. We went clubbing and raving. Me trying to play hard to get so as not to lose him again. Him saying, 'Don't go changing, to try and please me. I'll take you just the way you are.'

This time, I didn't sleep with him. All that mattered to me was that I wasn't going to let him slip through my fingers this time around. So I gave him something else in the meantime.

It all happened so quickly. A whirlwind romance. He got down on one knee and proposed. Of course I said, 'Yes.' It was what I wanted wasn't it?

Well, I wasn't sure to be honest.

I had got the man I wanted. The man who made my head spin and my tummy twist. The man who could make my heart skip a beat. But what you want, you can't get, and when you get it you wonder what all the fuss was about. There was something missing. M-A-G-I-C.

It wasn't his fault. There was nothing wrong with him. It was me. Or so I thought. I had my doubts right up to the night before the wedding. But then something happened. Something I can't explain. It was late at night. After hours of twisting and turning with worry about tying the knot in the morning,

I finally managed to doze off. I fell into a deep slumber. That night I dreamt of Leo. Only this time, the magic was there.

I dreamt he used the key I had given him to let himself into the flat. Just the touch of his hands made me gasp. His lips stroked every inch of my body. Each kiss was like heaven. It felt so good. And then we made love. Real love. For what seemed like hours. Better than any love I had ever had. It was pure magic.

I woke up at daybreak. Drenched in sweat. My hands between my thighs. Smelling of sex. My dream so vivid I could taste it. I couldn't stop thinking about it. Even as I joined Leo at the altar of All Saints Church later that morning. I wasn't anxious any longer. I was now sure that Leo still had that magic he had always had. We exchanged vows:

MY FIRST, MY LAST, MY ALL
YOU'RE MY SUN, MY MOON,
I KNOW THERE'S ONLY,
ONLY ONE LIKE YOU. NO WAY
COULD GOD HAVE MADE TWO

The wedding photos show that my folks were there at the church. On Leo's side it was just a few of his fellow officers.

Think of my shock when Trevor showed up at the reception. Leo had never mentioned him. Yet I knew straight away that I had married the wrong brother.

*   *   *

Trevor seemed just as surprised at seeing me.

'Do you two know each other?' Leo asked.

Trevor looked to me for an answer. I don't know why, I quickly said, 'No.' I know, I shouldn't have. But there were so many things going on in my head. My world was spinning fast. My life was upside down. I felt dizzy. It was making me feel sick. It was Trevor that I was in love with. But how could I tell Leo that, and so soon after the wedding? It would break his heart.

I was caught between a rock and a hard place and thought what Leo didn't know wouldn't hurt him. Now I've got to tell him I'm pregnant and I don't know who the father is.

12

THE MOTHER'S STORY

The truth will end my life.

It wasn't an easy choice to make. No mother should have to choose between her children but what was I to do? The twins had no life with me and my life wasn't worth living with them. Even though I felt nothing for them they were still mine. I was aware of that the whole time. Giving them up wasn't easy. But it was the only chance we had.

It's not the twins fault I never loved them. They are their father's sons. I look at them and I see Harry Hibbert. His face and his hate in their eyes. How could I love them? They were the product of a drunken rage that turned into a brutal rape.

At first I could not bring myself to touch them. They called it post-natal stress. But I knew it wasn't. I knew what it was. They were born to remind me of that assault. It was over a year before it was confirmed that I was going through a kind of breakdown. By then I was on my own with the twins. I was not able to make ends meet.

I got myself a job in a restaurant. That's where I met Roddy Charles. He was charming, dashing and madly in love with me. I could see it in his eyes. He was the best thing that had happened to me in a long time. The answer to my prayers. He was the knight in shining armour that would lift me from the nightmare I was living.

But I couldn't tell him the truth. I didn't get the feeling he would want the baggage. So I said nothing about Harry. And I didn't mention the kids.

In fact I became a new person. I told Roddy I was an orphan with no near kin. That I had returned home after living for many years overseas. Dizzy with love he saw no reason to dispute this. Even though his mother always hinted that she never quite believed me. But she's long gone. I've been married for nearly thirty years now.

I have a new family. Three lovely daughters June, April and May. They are the apples of my eye. They are my main concern. May is still only eighteen. I have to think about her. None of them know about my former life. It's been a big secret. I have to protect them. They are everything to me. I would die for them. I would kill for them.

Then there's my husband. Think what this could do to him if it came out. I had always hoped that someday I would be able to get the boys back and they would come and live with us in our large house. But it wasn't to be. The more success my husband had, the less likely it became. He went on to be a QC, then a judge and now he's a Law Lord. If someone was to find out about my former life it would be a scandal. It would kill Roddy to know that I've lied to him all this time.

So I had no contact with Trevor and Leo for years. Though I had heard through the grapevine that Trevor was living a life of crime and that Leo had joined the police force. It was Leo who tracked me down after many months of chasing leads. I wasn't too happy when he followed me from my house and challenged me in Harrods. I confessed. It was I, his mother. But begged him to be discrete.

He promised he would for the sake of his half-sisters, if I agreed to meet up with him because he had a lot of questions to ask me about us. He mostly wanted to know why I gave him up. So I told him what he needed to know, nothing more. I didn't mention Trevor and only talked about his father when he brought it up.

It was then that Leo told me about the dream. I panicked. I knew what it meant, but I dismissed it straight away. Told him not to mention it in case people thought he was cuckoo. Even now, I can't believe that someone can have a memory of something that happened when they were just two-years-old.

So I kept in touch with Leo to make sure that his dream stayed a secret. And it would have because he enjoys being with me and seems to trust me. He confides in me. He phoned me the day he fell in love. He sent me an e-mail the day he proposed. He tells me all his secrets. That's why I know which buttons to push to make him explode.

I would never have told Leo about his brother if it hadn't been for the story in the papers. It was Leo who made contact with Trevor in prison. Told him all. Trevor threatened to expose me if I didn't go and visit him in jail. So I went undercover. When he saw me, he wept. Like a baby. Said he had always wanted to hold his mother. Just once.

I cried too when Trevor said he forgave me. Said he still loved me. I embraced him.

He asked the same questions as Leo. I gave the same answers. He promised to keep my secret. But he wanted to keep contact. I gave him my e-mail.

That's how I found out about his dream. Behind bars he had time on his hands. He wrote rambling e-mails filling me in on all the gruesome details of his life of crime and what had happened to him over the years. In one exchange after a few months, Trevor mentioned the dreams that he has been having all his life. His dream was like Leo's, with one difference. Trevor saw the man falling over the cliff from the other point of view. Trevor didn't see the man with the moustache and the trilby. Instead he saw me shoving someone or something over the cliff.

I nearly collapsed when I read that. I knew then that I had to do something drastic to make sure that Leo and Trevor never told each other their dreams. That the two pieces of the jigsaw would never join.

I didn't mean to kill Harry. But how much abuse can a woman take. He came home drunk and shouting. I was at the top of the stairs. The children were in my arms and they were frightened. I told Harry to calm down but he wouldn't. He raised his voice some more and climbed up the stairs to teach me a lesson.

It was the hardest punch I ever felt. Right in my eye. I tell you, my sight has never been the same since. I fell to the floor and was stunned for a second. When I woke, I saw Leo and Trevor on the ground. I had dropped them. They were crying. And just at that moment I saw a flash come towards my head.

If I hadn't caught Harry by the ankle he would have kicked my head in. He lost balance and fell backwards, down the stairs. He lay there stone cold dead.

Only then did I realise what I had done. I knew I was in trouble. I panicked. As if it had just dawned on me that killing someone was a crime. It was self-defence, but would anyone believe me?

His eyes staring up at me, the twins crying.

I still had one problem to deal with straight away. How to dispose of the body. But you really don't want to hear about that. That was the most gruesome part of all. Leo's always saying 'people don't just vanish.'

Except they do. Every day. And Harry has vanished never to be found.

Leo and Trevor dream the death of their father every night. Somehow I have to make sure that they never talk about it. That's why I sent the e-mail. Leo will never know it came from me. That was how he found out that Trevor had been with his wife.

It was a stroke of luck really. I hired a private eye to follow him from prison. When he called to say Trevor was at Jenny's address, I knew there would be trouble. I didn't want them to kill each other, though. All I wanted to do was make sure they fell out with each other. I wanted them to not trust each other so much.

I wanted them to become like strangers to each other, so they would not share each other's secrets. Just to hate each other enough that the last thing they would do is tell each other their dreams.

The more I think about how much I have to lose, the more I realise that it would be better if one of them did kill the other. It's a terrible thing for a mother to say, but what else can I do? Leo is in the police force. He solves riddles for a living.

13

HARRY'S STORY

Do you believe in ghosts? No, really. Do you believe in spirits? Have you ever felt a chill go through you late on a hot summer's night? Have you seen your curtains rustle even when there's no wind? And what about the creaking of a floorboard that you couldn't explain? It always seems to happen at night, doesn't it?

That's when the spooks all come out. At night when there's no-one else around. Have you heard a haunting whisper from behind when you were trying to sleep in a strange house or in a graveyard on a dark night? And when you turned around you found you were all alone?

I said, do you believe in ghosts? Have you ever seen one? Or have you ever seen something that you couldn't explain? Has the face of a dearly departed ever come back to haunt you, so real you could almost touch it? If I told you I've seen a ghost would you believe me?

What about life after death? Do you believe that a dead man can come back to life? I know it's a scary thing to think about, but has a dead person ever let you know that they are there, watching you. You don't believe in ghosts? No, I never used to either. I know what you're thinking, 'if ghosts exist, show me the proof'.

Like you, I never believed in anything that couldn't be proved. I never believed in ghosts and I never believed in God. But I do now. You see, I've got the proof. I'm the living proof. You see, I know all about ghosts. And I know they exist. I know, because I am a ghost.

No seriously, I'm a kind of ghost. I died and I came back. Maybe I'm still dead. I'm not sure. My name is Harry Hibbert. Or should that be 'was, Harry Hibbert'? Yes, I'm Leo and Trevor's dad. Their mum murdered me. It was nearly thirty years ago now. She thinks she's gotten away with it. But she hasn't. Even if it takes thirty more years, she's going to pay for what she did. She 'killed' me for no reason at all. She robbed me of my best years and deprived my sons of their father.

Our marriage was never a happy one. From the start her folks didn't approve of her hitching up with someone like me. They were full of airs. They felt that their daughter could have done better for herself, and they never stopped letting me know that. As far as they were concerned I couldn't put a foot right. Even though I did all I could for my wife. After a while, you start hating your in-laws as much as they dislike you.

We have a saying where I'm from, 'it takes trash to know trash'. Maria's mother and father never stopped letting her know that they hoped for better from her.

Even though she was no better than me, after a while of folks saying the same thing over and over again, you start to believe it too, I guess. I began to see it in her eyes that Maria also thought she had married beneath herself. But I loved my wife. Until she started sounding like her folks.

The older she got the more she became like them. She was never happy with what I could provide. I got a good job. I worked all the hours that God gave and she would still complain that we never lived in a big house or had a flash car or went on trips abroad. It could have been so sweet and dandy between us. But she was always looking for someone better. I really was trying my best, you know. I knew I wasn't perfect. But I was trying, even with so many people against me. Then she got pregnant and had the kids, and that's when our marriage really started falling apart.

We hadn't planned for two kids in one go. It's hard enough trying to provide for one child, let alone two. So you can figure how I felt when two children came out instead of one. If we were struggling with money before, it was going to get worse now that was for sure. And it did. It was like Maria no longer trusted me. She started quizzing me and checking up on me. Where I had been, where I was going, where I was coming from. A woman's not supposed to be asking a man those kinda things.

Our marriage went from bad to worse, to worserer. But she was my wife. For better or worse. I took the good times, so I was going to take the bad times. The only thing I couldn't accept was how she hated the kids. She wasn't looking after them as she should have. Above all Trevor. Or was it Leo? I forget.

I would come back from work sometimes and see the kids by themselves in the house. No sign of Maria. How can you leave a baby by itself in a house? What kind of a mother are you when you behave like that, eh? I don't know what was up with her.

It was like she couldn't really deal with being a mother. I mean from the moment she gave birth, she didn't want to hold her babies. She would start freaking out like she was going to die if they came any nearer. She couldn't stand the sight of them. And then it was like she blamed me for the babies, so she couldn't stand the sight of me either.

It happened so quickly and yet so slowly. It was like inch-by-inch and step-by-step. But I never saw the change in her until it was too late. I mean a mother's supposed to stay at home with her kids, isn't she?

One night I came home and one of the twins had crawled up to an open window, and was balancing there on the ledge. I only just managed to catch him before he fell. That was it. I had had enough. I wasn't going to take any more chances. I hugged my babies tight, and thanked the Lord. Then I made the vow that I would never leave the twins with their unfit mother again.

With a twin in each arm I was on my way out of the house when their mother arrived. She gave me a look like she couldn't be bothered. Until I told her that I planned to get my babies as far away from her as possible. Then she flipped. I was like 'I'm leaving.' She was like, 'Oh no you're not!'

She started screaming and effing and blinding, like she was going to kill me. She lost it big time. I took the babies back upstairs to their bedroom so they didn't have to see any of this.

I really didn't need any more drama. Maria was waiting for me on the landing. She screamed at me again, 'You bastard. I won't let you take my babies from me.'

The next thing I knew she hurtled herself towards me with a knife in her hand. 'You crazy or what?' I screamed and took a step back to avoid her and went tumbling down the stairs. Head first. I must have broken my neck. Either way, I died.

That's for sure. I know I was dead, because my wife came running down the stairs and felt my pulse, and started sobbing and repeating over and over again, 'I killed him, oh God, I killed my husband.'

She held me to her chest mumbling 'Don't die. Please don't die, Harry. Please don't die. Don't leave me.'

I don't know how, but I saw the whole thing happening. I watched from above. I saw me lying there with my broken neck. I saw my wife sobbing. I looked up and saw the twins at the top of the stairs looking down. I knew I was dead. But then again I wasn't.

So do you believe in ghosts now? You don't have to, really you don't. But I suppose, like most people, you like a good ghost story. Am I right? Okay then, let me tell you mine. There was this time when I heard the dancing of footsteps and laughter and the playing of old fashioned music upstairs in my house when I was the only one at home.

Then there was the time when my dog went crazy in the living room, barking at an empty armchair. And attacking the thin air above it, as if he had grabbed someone with his teeth. I was young then and even though I felt the skin creeping along the back of my neck, I refused to believe in ghosts.

I recall when I hitchhiked and got a lift from this strange woman in a car. I was sitting in the front seat next to her and I must have fallen asleep. I was jolted awake by the driving and when I looked beside me, there was no one there. I wiped the sleep from my eyes, and looked again, and there she was smiling this strange sickly smile that seemed a thousand years old. Somehow I knew the person sitting next to me was no longer living. But there was nothing I could about it.

So there I was, lying dead on the ground. With my wife weeping and wailing. I watched as she quickly got over her sorrow and figured out a plan. We had a cellar in that old house. My wife dragged me to the hatch and threw me down. Well, even if I wasn't dead before, I was now. It was a drop of 15 or so feet. My body went down head first. The fall smashed my skull. I stayed there with my body laying there for a few days before the next thing happened. The hatch door opened and a gush of cement poured in on top of me. And it kept coming and coming. Well, I thought that was the end of me. I could see Maria's plan. And I knew that no one would ever know what had happened to me.

I was a goner. Or so I thought. I don't know what happened next, I really don't. I can't explain it. All I can say is that I came to life again. Despite the broken neck and the smashed skull, clothes all dirty, nose all bloody.

'No, don't bury me! I'm not dead!' I screamed over and over without a single sound. Then I was sure I was dead. Or maybe I wasn't. I knew what was going on. I could feel the cement filling up the cellar. I was swimming in it. And I panicked. A stench filled the stifling air. I was shitting myself.

I couldn't get up, I could barely flinch. But you won't believe what a man can do when he is desperate. I heard a voice say, 'No one will ever hear you. No one will ever see you. Unless you figure your way out.' This was no nightmare. There was no waking relief from my living death.

This was real.

My heart's every thump jumped out of my mouth as the blood sped through my veins. Surely I would suffer a heart attack and die in any case. Come friendly death, come. I wept. Please God, not this. No!

I couldn't think straight for fear. In a vain belief that I could force my way out I began to wade through the tons of ready mix. Somehow, I clawed my way out of that cellar, brick-by-brick as the cement filled up all around me. I don't have any other idea of what happened after that. I must have lost my mind. And when I regained my senses I was in a home, in the care of the local council out here in Luton. I was able to build a new life for myself.

I have a wife now, a son and two lovely daughters. He's a copper on the local force and he's called Harry just like his Dad. My past life had been a memory from the grave until the day Leo came to my door.

Something told me that Leo would be calling at my door that very day. Recently I told my wife Sheila, about my previous life. It wasn't easy and she was not happy that I'd kept such a secret from her. But the truth is that I'd only recently worked out what happened to me all those years ago.

I told her that for the sake of our happy family she would have to invent a story that I had left her nearly thirty years ago. This was the story she would tell if either Leo or Trevor ever came looking for me.

It broke my heart that Sunday afternoon when Leo called. I watched him, concealed at the top of the stairs. It may be a cruel thing to have done to Leo, but there are some ghosts that are best left in the grave.

I'm a ghost. Walking through the wind with a bottle of gin, thinking about things that could have been, would have been, should have been.

I wipe my tears, because real ghosts don't cry. I haven't got any fears. I wish good luck to my sons, but their mum's going to get what she deserves. I haunt her every night. She hasn't had a decent night's sleep in years. I'll haunt her until her dying days. I'm the creak that keeps her up all night. I'm the howl she can hear in her ears. I'm the one who is keeping her restless. I'm the ghost in her mind. I am a ghost, who walks with the living. Who lives and breathes.